The Dirtiest Minivan in the world

Bridget Brennan

Tellwell Talent
www.tellwell.ca

ISBN
978-0-2288-4895-0 (Hardcover)
978-0-2288-4894-3 (Paperback)
978-0-2288-4896-7 (eBook)

Dedications

For Brian, Evabel, Jesse and Clarey for this crazy ride.

......how did this happen??????

A Sweet New Ride

One sunny summer day, while expecting twin boys to arrive at any moment, Eva's mommy and daddy bought a brand spanking new grey minivan and drove it home, with three brand new car seats perfectly installed.

It was spotless, it smelled fresher than a clean baby's bum, and it was OH SO CLEAN!!!

The Forgotten Diaper Change

The twins were born, and everyone drove home from the hospital in the shiny new van. However, as weeks passed, Eva's mommy or daddy would have to do an emergency diaper change in the trunk of the minivan.

Sometimes, an immediate place to throw away the diaper wasn't available, so the diaper was folded up, placed under a seat, and occasionally...forgotten.

Animal Fur Ambush

While frequenting the beach and the park with their two dogs, three small humans, three strollers, diaper bag and supplies, Eva's mommy and daddy forgot that the dogs were completely filthy after each visit, and they failed to clean them off before letting them in the van.

Animal fur starting drifting like tumbleweeds all over the van...

Visions of Vomit

While taking a little family trip, Eva's mommy and daddy gave her a tablet to play games on. As Eva played, she started to feel a little bit funny, and as her eyes closed, her belly heaved, and she threw up all over the car (*and all over her twin brothers!*).

Eva's mommy tried to clean it up as best as she could, but a bit of the smell continued to linger...

Land of the Loose and Lone Socks

Rather strangely, Eva's family minivan started acting like a washer and dryer, and began eating just one sock at a time, leaving the other sock alone and useless.

Eva's mommy and daddy didn't know why there were so many socks in the mini-van to begin with, as a mini-van isn't a typical place to take off socks, yet this great mystery remains unsolved, and the lone socks continued to collect in the van.

Juice Pack and Sippy Cup Junkyard

Juice packs and sippy cups with milk were often given to the thirsty toddlers in the van. This critical error frequently resulted in juice all over the floor and milk all over the mats, creating a sticky and slimy sensation to anyone who dared step foot in the back seat.

Crazy Cracker Crumbs

Eva's mommy and daddy made the unforgiveable mistake of feeding the children snacks in the minivan to try and stop their constant crying, whinging and whining, and massive meltdowns with offerings of crackers, chips and cookies.

Occasionally, Eva's family dogs would eat the leftover snacks, but even they were shocked by the sheer abundance of crumbs.

Car Seat Stuffing

Slowly, all three of the children's car seats began losing their stuffing. It was so odd! Handfuls of stuffing sprinkled and scattered all over the van!

Eva's daddy guessed that the dogs had ripped the stuffing out while trying to eat cracker crumbs, but he really wasn't sure......

Squirrel Squalor

Sometimes, Eva's mommy or daddy would **forget** to close the sliding van door and not notice this error until the following morning. The minivan stayed open for business **ALL NIGHT LONG.**

Unfortunately, this meant that a family of enterprising squirrels slowly moved into the van, eating first the engine, then getting into the roof and eating the electrical lines, and finally eating the minivan floor.

The squirrels had taken advantage of the squalor inside the minivan, and Eva's family minivan officially became…

THE DIRTIEST MINIVAN IN THE WORLD

A Dirty Departure

...The next day, the tow truck came and took the minivan away.

It was beyond repair, and it found a permanent home in a junkyard where it is now an extremely dirty residence to the family of squirrels, all of their extended family, many mice, a few raccoons, and even a grumpy groundhog.

Eva's family purchased a NEW minivan (and new car seats), and as they drove it home, Eva's daddy remarked that it was 'OH SO CLEAN!"...)

Manufactured by Amazon.ca
Bolton, ON

21013479R00017